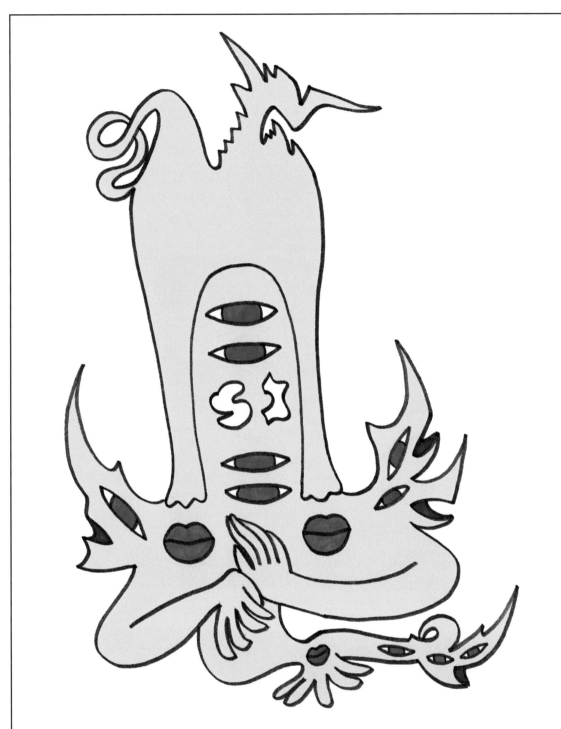

Prakatar

Prakatar, Royal Master of Realms, proclaimed the Maragan to Kings Sokhen and Sokhit.

Sokhen

Promising him a reward if he revealed the way to the Speckled Foot of Infinite Pleasure, Prakatar unveiled the realm's portal.

Sokhit

Granting him the title Second King, he blessed them with a solemn farewell, and they went through the portal to the Realm of Maragan.

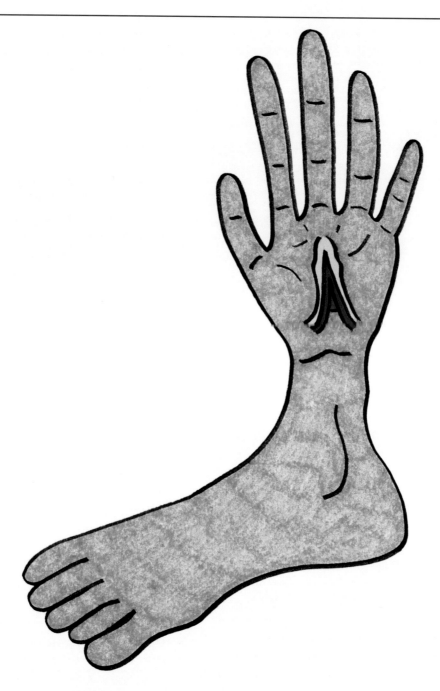

Maragan Realm Creature

Descending from the sky, Sokhen and Sokhit explored the wondrouslands until they came to a mysterious door, which the two men subdued and went inside.

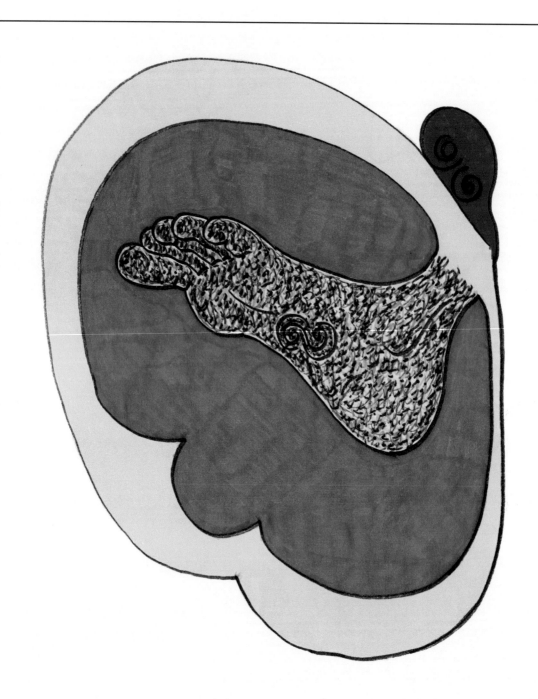

Maragan

Marveling at the vast multitude, both Kings went into them and became defiled. Finding the Maragan in one of numerous rooms, Sokhen and Sokhit approached the splendid foot.

Andevi

Magnificently, the Maragan vanished before their eyes. Both men were appalled by its disappearance and immediately they left the realm's interior. Waiting for them outside, Andevi, Jade Princess, cast them into Queensridge without hesitance.

NeoKhmer Red Queensridge

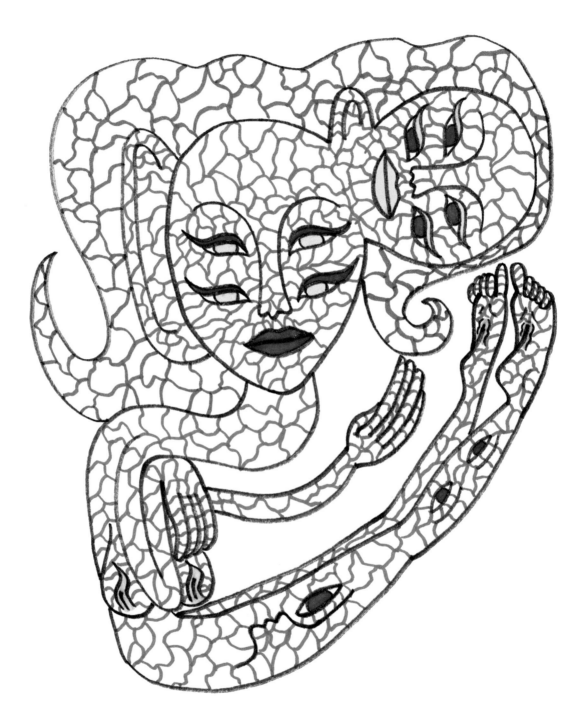

NeoKhmer Blue Queensridge

Order this book online at www.trafford.com
or email orders@trafford.com

Most Trafford titles are also available at major online book retailers.

 www.trafford.com

North America & international
toll-free: 844 688 6899 (USA & Canada)
fax: 812 355 4082

Our mission is to efficiently provide the world's finest, most
comprehensive book publishing service, enabling every author to
experience success. To find out how to publish your book, your way,
and have it available worldwide, visit us online at www.trafford.com

ISBN: 978-1-4251-2119-8

Print information available on the last page.

Trafford rev. 03/10/2021

Printed in the United States
by Baker & Taylor Publisher Services